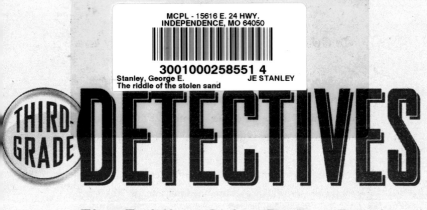

THIRD-GRADE DETECTIVES

The Riddle of the Stolen Sand

By **GEORGE E. STANLEY**

Illustrated by **SALVATORE MURDOCCA**

ALADDIN · New York London Toronto Sydney New Delhi

To Gwen, James, and Charles, with all my love.

First Aladdin Paperbacks edition February 2003
Text copyright © 2003 by George Edward Stanley
Illustrations copyright © 2003 by Salvatore Murdocca

ALADDIN PAPERBACKS
An imprint of Simon & Schuster Children's Publishing Division
1230 Avenue of the Americas, New York, NY 10020

Also available in an Aladdin library edition.
Designed by Steve Scott
The text for this book was set in 12-point Lino Letter.
Manufactured in the United States of America
8 10 9

The Library of Congress Control Number for the library edition is
2002107704
ISBN-13: 978-0-689-85376-0   ISBN-10: 0-689-85376-9
0819 OFF

Chapter One

It was Friday morning.

Noelle Trocoderro and Todd Sloan were walking to school.

When they turned a corner, they saw the sheriff's car parked in front of Mr. Roper's grocery store.

"Let's check it out!" Noelle said.

She and Todd started running.

Noelle was always looking for mysteries to solve.

Their teacher, Mr. Merlin, called their class the Third-Grade Detectives.

Just as Noelle and Todd reached the front of the grocery store, the sheriff and another man came outside.

The sheriff was carrying a big box.

"I'll teach you to steal from me, Roper!" the man was shouting. "I'll see you in court! You're going to jail for a long time!"

At that moment, Mr. Roper appeared at the door. "You're full of hot air, Williams!" he shouted back at the man. "You can't prove this, because it didn't happen!"

Mr. Williams waved his fist at Mr. Roper. "You just wait and see! Your grocery store will soon belong to me!"

The sheriff and Mr. Williams got into the car and drove off.

Mr. Roper went back into his grocery store.

"This is terrible, Todd! We have to talk to Mr. Merlin right away!" Noelle said. "He'll know what to do."

When they got to their classroom, Mr. Merlin was writing some spelling words on the chalkboard.

"Mr. Merlin! Mr. Merlin!" Noelle shouted. "Mr. Williams is going to take Mr. Roper's grocery store away from him! He's going to send him to jail for a long time!"

Mr. Merlin stopped writing. "What?" he said.

"Mr. Williams said Mr. Roper stole something from him," Noelle explained. "But we don't believe him! Mr. Roper would never do anything like that!"

"It's a mystery, Mr. Merlin!" Todd said.

"Then maybe the Third-Grade Detectives can solve it," Mr. Merlin said.

The bell rang.

Noelle and Todd took their seats.

The rest of the class came into the room.

Noelle was sorry that Mr. Williams wanted to send Mr. Roper to jail.

But she was glad they had a mystery to solve.

Amber Lee Johnson will be so mad, Noelle thought.

Amber Lee always liked to find the mysteries for Mr. Merlin's Third-Grade Detectives to solve.

When everyone was seated, Mr. Merlin looked at Noelle. "Would you like to tell the class what happened this morning?"

Noelle stood up.

She described what she and Todd had seen.

Amber Lee gasped. She started waving her hand.

Noelle ignored her.

Amber Lee jumped out of her seat.

She looked really mad.

"This is *my* mystery, Mr. Merlin!" Amber Lee shouted.

Mr. Merlin looked puzzled.

"What do you mean, Amber Lee?" he asked her.

"My mother and I were *inside* Mr. Roper's grocery store when it happened," Amber Lee said.

Noelle looked really disappointed.

"We stopped there so my mother could buy some oysters for a party she's giving this weekend," Amber Lee said.

"Yuck!" Leon Dennis said. "Oysters are disgusting!"

Amber Lee gave him a dirty look.

"My mother bought three dozen oysters," Amber Lee continued.

"They were still in the shell.

"We had just started to leave when Mr. Williams arrived with the sheriff.

"Mr. Williams accused Mr. Roper of stealing oysters from him.

"He said he had *proof* and was going to bring criminal charges against Mr. Roper.

"Mr. Williams had a court order allowing the sheriff to take all of Mr. Roper's oysters.

"But Mr. Roper said he didn't steal the oysters from Mr. Williams.

"He said he *bought* them from Mr. Spencer's oyster farm."

Mr. Merlin thought for a minute. "This is very interesting, class," he said. "Mr. Williams owns an oyster farm on North Bay, fifty miles *north* of town, and Mr. Spencer owns an oyster farm on South Bay, fifty miles *south* of town."

"Did your mother give the sheriff the oysters she bought?" Todd asked.

"Of course not! She had already paid for them!" Amber Lee said. "She needs them for her party!"

"Why did they take Mr. Roper's oysters?" Misty Goforth asked.

"Evidence," Amber Lee replied.

That's strange! Noelle thought. *How can oysters be evidence?*

Chapter Two

"We need to solve the mystery, Mr. Merlin!" Noelle said. "We have to prove that Mr. Roper didn't steal those oysters!"

"But what if he did?" Todd asked. "A detective should always keep an open mind."

"Mr. Roper gives kids candy when they're shopping with their parents, Todd!" Misty said. "He would never steal anything!"

"He gives me ice cream," Leon added. "I like that better than candy!"

"Todd's right, class," Mr. Merlin said. "Detectives can't take sides.

"We'll try to solve the mystery, but first, we need to do our science lesson."

The class groaned.

"But we're going to study bivalve mollusks

today," Mr. Merlin said. "So we might learn something that will help you solve the mystery about Mr. Roper."

Noelle was puzzled.

She raised her hand.

"What do *bivalve mollusks* have to do with Mr. Roper?" she asked.

Mr. Merlin smiled. "That's what oysters are, Noelle," he said. "So are clams and mussels.

"Bivalve means they have two sides called valves. Some people also call them shells.

"The shells are held together by a piece of skin called a ligament."

Mr. Merlin held up a picture for them to see.

He told them that bivalves had been around for more than five hundred million years.

He told them that there were more than six thousand types of bivalves.

"People eat the insides," Mr. Merlin said, "but the shells are important too.

"We use them to make buttons.

"We grind them up to help make roads."

Amber Lee raised her hand.

"Yes, Amber Lee," Mr. Merlin said.

"Oysters also make pearls," she said. "I know how they do it too!"

"Would you like to tell us?" Mr. Merlin asked.

Amber Lee nodded.

She walked to the front of the room.

"Sometimes a grain of sand gets inside the oyster," she began.

"It makes the oyster mad, because the sand scratches!

"The same thing happens to me when I go to the beach.

"I get sand between my toes and in my hair and it makes me so mad, because I have to . . ."

"Amber Lee, please tell us about pearls," Mr. Merlin said.

"Well, I can take a bath," Amber Lee continued, "but the oyster can't.

"So the oyster starts covering the grain of sand with smooth stuff so it won't scratch anymore.

"That smooth stuff becomes a pearl."

"Thank you, Amber Lee," Mr. Merlin said. "That was a very good explanation.

"The smooth stuff is called *nacre*. Sometimes it's white. Sometimes it's gray.

"Just as Amber Lee said, it builds up in layers around the grain of sand and forms a pearl."

Leon raised his hand.

"Maybe Mr. Roper stole the oysters to see if they had pearls in them," he said.

"Mr. Roper is not a thief!" Amber Lee said.

Mr. Merlin sighed.

"I can tell that our minds are still on Mr. Roper," he said. He closed the science book.

"I'm going to give you a secret code clue," he said.

Noelle got excited.

When Mr. Merlin gave them secret codes, they were on their way to solving a mystery.

Mr. Merlin used to be a spy.

He used to crack lots of secret codes.

He told the Third-Grade Detectives that figuring out secret codes made them think better.

"We're ready, Mr. Merlin!" Noelle said.

Mr. Merlin started writing on the chalkboard. He wrote:

L O A T E A D O K T H S N

Noelle studied the secret code clue carefully. She had to figure it out.

If she didn't, Mr. Roper might lose his grocery store!

Chapter Three

The lunch bell rang.

"Let's work on the secret code clue while we eat," Todd said.

"Okay," Noelle said. "But it really looks hard."

They headed for the cafeteria.

Amber Lee already had her tray.

She was sitting with Leon and Misty.

"Amber Lee thinks I stole her mystery," Noelle said. "She'll try to solve the secret code clue before we do."

Noelle and Todd got their trays.

"I hope we don't have oysters today," Todd said. "I saw my uncle eat an oyster once. He slurped it down."

"We've never had oysters before, Todd," Noelle said. "Why would we have them today?"

"Have you forgotten, Noelle?" Todd said. "Sometimes Mr. Merlin gets the cafeteria to serve our class what we're studying."

"Oh, yeah," Noelle said.

They had eaten octopus.

They had eaten rattlesnake.

Noelle looked down the cafeteria line.

Mrs. Caruthers was helping serve today.

Suddenly, Noelle had a great idea.

If it worked, they wouldn't have to solve the secret code clue.

Noelle loved Mrs. Caruthers.

Mrs. Caruthers had been her baby-sitter before Noelle started school.

She always cooked whatever Noelle wanted to eat.

"Yes! Hamburgers and french fries!" Todd said. "My favorite!"

Mrs. Caruthers handed Todd his plate.

Noelle pretended to look at the hamburgers.

"Mrs. Caruthers, do you have any oysters?" she asked. "That's what I'm really hungry for."

Todd gave Noelle a funny look.

So did Mrs. Caruthers. *Oysters?* she said.

Noelle nodded.

Mrs. Caruthers thought for a minute.

"You know something?" she said. "I think we do have a can of oysters around here somewhere.

"But it's probably been on the pantry shelf for months."

Mrs. Caruthers looked around to see if anyone else was watching them.

"I guess I could open it for you," she said.

Mrs. Caruthers called another worker to serve the hamburgers.

Noelle and Todd stepped aside to let the students behind them pass.

In a few minutes, Mrs. Caruthers returned with a bowl. She handed it to Noelle.

Noelle's stomach suddenly felt funny.

The bowl was full of gray shiny things that shook when she moved the bowl.

Mrs. Caruthers gave Noelle a big smile. "Enjoy!" she said.

Noelle and Todd headed for an empty table.

"Are you going to *eat* that?" Todd asked.

"Of course not, Todd," Noelle said. "This is evidence."

"What do you mean?" Todd asked.

Noelle set her tray down on the table. "Mr. Roper was arrested because of oysters, Todd. I want to see if I can find out why," she said.

"I'm going to examine these oysters like a police scientist would."

Noelle took her fork.

She started moving the oysters around.

They slid all over each other.

Noelle's stomach felt funny again.

She took a deep breath.

She was sure that police scientists didn't get sick when they looked at evidence.

She wouldn't get sick either.

She looked and looked at the oysters.

She moved them around and around.

Nothing.

"What are you doing, Noelle?"

Noelle looked up.

Amber Lee was standing behind her.

"Hey! Those are oysters!" Amber Lee cried. "I didn't know we could have oysters for lunch!"

"I'm not eating them, Amber Lee," Noelle whispered. "I'm trying to solve the mystery."

Amber Lee stamped her foot.

"We're supposed to solve the secret code clue!" she shouted. "We're not supposed to look at oysters!"

Several other kids stared at them.

Amber Lee took a deep breath. "Did you solve the code?" she asked.

"No," Noelle said.

"Good!" Amber Lee said.

Noelle and Todd watched as Amber Lee, Leon, and Misty left the cafeteria.

Noelle moved the oysters around again.

But she still didn't see anything that would prove Mr. Roper innocent.

"I think you need to stop looking at those oysters and help me solve the secret code clue," Todd said.

He spread a piece of paper out on the table.

"I don't recognize this code," he said.

Noelle looked. "Me neither," she said. "Come on! If nobody has solved it, Mr. Merlin will give us a hint."

They emptied their trays and headed back to their classroom.

Chapter Four

"Has anyone figured out the secret code clue yet?" Mr. Merlin asked.

No one raised a hand. No one had.

"Okay," Mr. Merlin said. "I'll give you a hint.

"This is called a Rail-Fence Code.

"Think about what we studied in history last week."

Noelle loved history.

She thought about last week.

They had studied about settlers.

They had studied how the settlers built fences around their land.

They cut down trees so they could plant their crops.

They used some of the logs to build their houses.

They split some logs into *rails* for corn cribs, hog pens, and *fences*.

They sometimes called the rail fences *worm* fences because they were crisscrossed in a zigzag fashion—just like a worm crawls.

Zigzag! Noelle thought. That's it!

She raised her hand.

"Yes, Noelle?" Mr. Merlin said.

"I think I can solve the secret code clue!" Noelle said.

The rest of the class groaned.

"I was just about to solve it too, Mr. Merlin!" Amber Lee said.

"Class! Class!" Mr. Merlin said. "Please be quiet."

The class settled down.

"Noelle raised her hand first," Mr. Merlin continued. "So she gets the first chance to solve the secret code clue."

Noelle walked to the front of the room.

She picked up a piece of chalk.

"I love history," she began. "I remember studying about rail fences."

She reminded the class about how rail fences were built.

She drew a picture of a rail fence on the board.

"That means this secret code will look like a rail fence," she explained.

She wrote the secret code on the chalkboard:

L O A T E A D   O K T H S N

"To decode this message, you take the first letter of the first word and you zigzag it with the first letter of the second word.

"You continue doing that until you have used all of the letters.

"It will look like this:

L   O   A   T   E   A   D
   O   K   T   H   S   N

"You zigzag when you read it too."

"Look at the sand!" the class shouted.

Noelle couldn't believe it.

She had wanted to say that.

But she had solved the secret code clue.

So she guessed that was good enough.

"Excellent, Noelle!" Mr. Merlin said.

Noelle went back to her seat.

"What sand?" Todd asked Mr. Merlin.

"That's something Mr. Merlin's Third-Grade Detectives will have to figure out," Mr. Merlin said.

"I know where there's lots of sand," Noelle whispered. "At the beach."

"Then that's where we need to go," Todd whispered back.

"My family is going tomorrow morning," Noelle said. "Do you want to come with us?"

"Yes!" Todd said. "We'll look at the sand and solve the mystery."

Chapter Five

Todd was at Noelle's house early the next morning.

He and Noelle helped Mr. and Mrs. Trocoderro pack their van.

An hour later, they pulled into the beach parking lot.

"Why is that fence over there?" Mrs. Trocoderro asked.

"That's where the public beach ends," Mr. Trocoderro said.

"There's an oyster farm on the other side."

Noelle looked at the fence.

There was a man working on it.

"Todd! Look!" Noelle whispered. "It's Mr. Williams!"

"You're right!" Todd whispered back.

"Mr. Merlin said, 'Look at the sand,'" Noelle reminded him.

"Mr. Williams accused Mr. Roper of stealing oysters from him.

"So Mr. Merlin must have been talking about Mr. Williams's sand.

"We'll get some of the sand from the beach in front of Mr. Williams's oyster farm and look at it."

"Good idea," Todd said.

"We're going to dig in the sand!" Noelle said to her parents.

She grabbed a bucket and a small shovel.

"Sounds like fun," Mrs. Trocoderro said.

Noelle and Todd headed toward the fence.

"Kids! Kids!" Mr. Trocoderro called to them. "Don't go past that fence!"

"We won't," Noelle said.

"How can we solve the mystery if we don't go past the fence?" Todd asked.

"Leave it to me," Noelle told him.

When they reached the fence, they sat down at the edge.

"What do you kids want?" Mr. Williams asked.

"Nothing. We're just playing in the sand,"

Noelle said. "We're going to build a castle."

"Well, you can't play on this side of the fence, so don't try," Mr. Williams warned.

"This beach is only for people who want to buy my oysters!

"It's not for people to play on!"

"Who would want to buy *his* oysters?" Noelle whispered to Todd.

"Yeah!" Todd agreed.

Noelle and Todd pretended to build a sand castle.

When Mr. Williams wasn't looking, Noelle stuck the small shovel through the wire fence and scooped up some of the sand.

She put it in the bucket.

"Come on," she said to Todd. "Let's go where he can't hear us."

They walked down the public beach.

They sat near the edge of the water and looked at the sand in the bucket.

"It just looks like sand," Todd said.

"I know," Noelle agreed. "What did Mr. Merlin's secret code clue mean?"

After a while, Todd started to empty the bucket.

"No!" Noelle said. "Don't do that!"

"Why not?" Todd asked.

"We'll ask Mr. Merlin for another secret code clue to help us solve the mystery.

"We may still need this sand."

Noelle put the bucket in the van.

Then she and Todd ran up and down the beach.

They looked for shells.

They made funny faces in the sand with their toes.

Finally, Mr. Trocoderro said, "Well, it's time to go home. Did you two have fun?"

Noelle and Todd nodded.

But Noelle knew it would have been even more fun if they had solved the mystery.

Chapter Six

On Sunday afternoon, Noelle said, "Let's look at Mr. Williams's sand again, Todd. We may have missed something the first time."

So they each scooped up a handful of sand and studied it.

"It still just looks like sand to me," Todd said.

"I know," Noelle agreed. "But we need to keep looking at it."

"Do you think we should count the grains?" Todd asked.

"Todd! There are billions and billions of grains of sand here," Noelle said. "Anyway, how would that keep Mr. Roper from going to jail?"

Todd shrugged. "I wonder if Amber Lee has solved the mystery."

"Let's go ask her," Noelle said. "We'll take the

bucket of sand just in case she says something that will give us a clue."

Amber Lee lived two blocks over from Noelle's house.

Todd rang the doorbell.

Amber Lee answered. She saw the bucket of sand. "What's that for?" she asked.

"Mr. Merlin said to look at the sand," Noelle said.

"Mr. Williams accused Mr. Roper of stealing oysters from him.

"So we got this sand from the beach at Mr. Williams's oyster farm.

"We've been looking at it."

"Did you solve the mystery?" Amber Lee asked.

Noelle and Todd shook their heads.

"Did you?" Noelle asked.

When Amber Lee didn't say anything, Todd said, "Amber Lee, Mr. Merlin wants us all to work together.

"That's important.

"We have to keep Mr. Roper from going to jail.

"We can't just think about who's going to be the first one to solve the mystery."

Amber Lee sighed. "Okay. Come to my room."

Noelle and Todd followed Amber Lee to her room.

When they got there, Noelle sniffed and said, "Yuck! What's that smell?"

Amber Lee looked around. "Is it really that bad? I even have the window open."

"Yes," Todd said. "It's awful."

Amber Lee closed the door. "It's oysters. The ones my mother got at Mr. Roper's grocery store."

"What are they doing in your room?" Noelle asked.

"My mother threw them away," Amber Lee said.

"Our refrigerator broke yesterday, and everything spoiled.

"I got the oysters out of the garbage so I could study them.

"I thought I could solve the mystery."

"Well?" Todd said. "Did you?"

Amber Lee sighed. "No," she said.

"Is your mother going to get some new oysters for her party?" Noelle asked.

Amber Lee nodded. "They just delivered our

new refrigerator. My mother's going down to South Bay to buy some from Mr. Spencer right now. Do you want to come with us?"

Noelle and Todd both said, "Yes!"

They called their parents.

Their parents said it was okay for them to go with Amber Lee and her mother to Mr. Spencer's oyster farm.

When they got there, Mr. Spencer and his wife were shucking oysters.

But Mrs. Spencer stopped to help Amber Lee's mother.

"Let's talk to Mr. Spencer about Mr. Roper," Noelle suggested.

Todd and Amber Lee thought that was a good idea.

"We want to keep Mr. Roper from going to jail," Noelle told Mr. Spencer. "We want to solve the mystery of the oysters."

"Well, I told the police that Mr. Roper bought his oysters from me," Mr. Spencer explained.

"But I was busy the day he came for them.

"He got them himself and said he'd send me a check later this week.

"I didn't even make out a receipt.

"He's an honest man.

"I knew he'd pay me.

"That's the way I do business sometimes.

"But there's really no proof that Mr. Roper bought the oysters from me."

Noelle, Todd, and Amber Lee were disappointed.

What were they going to do? Noelle wondered. Mr. Williams said he had *proof* that Mr. Roper stole the oysters from him.

Chapter Seven

The next morning at school, everyone looked really sad.

"Did anyone solve the mystery?" Mr. Merlin asked.

No one had.

"Did anyone figure out what the secret code clue meant?" Mr. Merlin asked.

No one had.

Noelle raised her hand.

"Yes, Noelle?" Mr. Merlin said.

"Todd and I got some sand from the beach at Mr. Williams's oyster farm.

"We looked and looked at it, but we didn't solve the mystery."

Amber Lee told Mr. Merlin about the trip they took to Mr. Spencer's oyster farm.

"Mr. Spencer was busy the day he sold his oysters to Mr. Roper. He didn't give Mr. Roper a receipt," she said.

"So there's no *proof* that Mr. Roper got his oysters from Mr. Spencer.

"And Mr. Williams said he has *proof* that Mr. Roper stole the oysters."

Mr. Merlin nodded. "I see," he said. "Well, I guess it's time for another secret code clue."

He turned around.

He started writing on the chalkboard.

He wrote:

E O S R I A E N   P C O C M R D U

It's probably another Rail-Fence Code! Noelle thought.

She rewrote the clue and zigzagged it like a rail fence:

E   O   S   R   I   A   E   N
  P   C   O   C   M   R   D   U

She zigzagged when she read it too.

She was just about to open her mouth when Amber Lee shouted, "Epocsorc Imarednu!"

Everyone started laughing.

"Class! Class! Don't laugh at Amber Lee!" Mr. Merlin said. "She recognized this as a Rail-Fence Code. That's exactly what it is."

"I recognized it too, Mr. Merlin!" Noelle said.

Several other kids said they did too.

"Okay! Okay! In a minute, I'll give you another hint," Mr. Merlin said. "But first let's talk about what we know so far."

"That's a good idea," Todd said.

"Mr. Williams accused Mr. Roper of stealing oysters from his oyster farm," Mr. Merlin began.

"Mr. Roper said he didn't do that. He said he bought them from Mr. Spencer's oyster farm.

"But Mr. Spencer was busy and didn't give Mr. Roper a receipt."

"Mr. Roper would never lie!" Misty Goforth said.

"We all believe that, Misty," Mr. Merlin said, "but we have to prove it.

"So now let's examine the *evidence* we have.

"Noelle and Todd got some sand from the

beach in front of Mr. Williams's oyster farm.

"Amber Lee's mother threw away the oysters that Mr. Williams said Mr. Roper stole from him.

"But Amber Lee dug them out of the garbage."

Mr. Merlin looked at Amber Lee. "Do you still have them?"

Amber Lee nodded. "I don't know how much longer I can keep them, though. My mother keeps asking me what that funny smell is in my room."

"Bring them to school," Mr. Merlin said. "I'll keep them safe for you."

Amber Lee looked relieved.

"Amber Lee's mother also bought some oysters from Mr. Spencer," Mr. Merlin said.

"Her guests didn't eat all of them at her party," Amber Lee said. "I'll ask Mother if I can have one of the leftovers for a school experiment."

"Good," Mr. Merlin said.

"Now I'll give you a hint which will help you solve this new secret code clue," he continued.

"*Turn the fence around.*"

Noelle looked at the secret code clue on the chalkboard.

If she turned the fence around, that meant what was on the left would be on the right, and what was on the right would be on the left.

She started reading:

"U N D E R . . . *Under!*"

She read the rest of the secret code clue. ". . . a microscope."

She thought for a minute.

Finally, she raised her hand.

"Yes, Noelle?" Mr. Merlin said.

"Look at the sand under a microscope!" Noelle said.

"Excellent," Mr. Merlin said.

"What sand?" Leon asked.

"Think about the evidence," Mr. Merlin said. "You have sand everywhere!"

That's right! Noelle thought. Now she knew exactly how they were going to solve this mystery.

Chapter Eight

"We're going to Dr. Smiley's house after school," Noelle announced to everyone at recess.

The class thought that was a great idea.

"I was going to say that too," Amber Lee said.

Dr. Smiley was a friend of Mr. Merlin's.

She was also a police scientist.

Dr. Smiley used science to solve crimes.

The Third-Grade Detectives had started a Dr. Smiley fan club.

Amber Lee was president.

Once a month, they'd meet at Dr. Smiley's house.

They'd have cookies and milk.

Amber Lee would talk on and on about what she planned to do when she became a police scientist.

After that, Dr. Smiley would tell them about a recent crime she had solved.

She would show them how she used science to do it.

"We'll take all of our evidence to her," Noelle said. "Dr. Smiley will let us use her microscopes."

Dr. Smiley had a police lab in the basement of her house.

She used it when she needed to work on a crime after she left her office.

Noelle could hardly wait until school was over.

But the day seemed to drag.

They had to do math.

They had to do spelling.

They even had to go to the auditorium to watch the kindergartners hop around in bunny costumes.

Noelle thought they looked sort of silly.

Then she remembered that she had done the same thing when she was in kindergarten.

Noelle wondered if, back then, some third grader had been sitting in the audience thinking that she looked silly too.

She suddenly felt embarrassed.

Finally, the bell rang.

Todd and Noelle hurried to Noelle's house.

Todd called his grandmother and told her what they were planning to do.

Todd's grandmother was a teacher's helper in the other third grade at his school.

But in the afternoon, she stayed at Todd's house until his parents got home from work.

Noelle went to her closet and got the pail of sand they had scooped up from the beach in front of Mr. Williams's oyster farm.

"We have our evidence, Todd," Noelle said. "Let's go!"

They rode their bicycles to Dr. Smiley's house.

It was three blocks on the other side of the school.

When they got there, they rang the bell.

Misty answered the door.

"We're all in the kitchen," she said. "We're having cookies and milk."

Noelle liked Dr. Smiley's cookies.

They weren't homemade, but they were always some of the best ones you could buy in a store.

"I see you brought your evidence," Dr. Smiley

said when Noelle and Todd came into the kitchen. "I'll take it to the lab while you have some cookies and milk."

Noelle handed Dr. Smiley the evidence.

Then she and Todd helped themselves to cookies and milk.

Noelle took one peanut butter and one oat-meal raisin.

Just as she finished the oatmeal raisin, Dr. Smiley's doorbell rang.

"That must be Amber Lee," Dr. Smiley called up to them. "She's the only member of the fan club who isn't here."

"I'll let her in," Noelle said. "She has evidence too."

"Something terrible has happened," Amber Lee announced when Noelle opened the door.

"What?" Todd asked.

Amber Lee held up a plastic bag.

It had one oyster in it.

"This is an oyster that my mother bought from Mr. Spencer's oyster farm," she said.

"But I don't have the oysters she bought at Mr. Roper's grocery store."

"Why not?" Noelle asked.

"Mother found them in my room. They were really smelling up the house!" Amber Lee said.

"She put them in the garbage.

"The garbage men picked up the garbage before I got home."

Dr. Smiley had just come back into the kitchen.

"That's too bad, Amber Lee," she said. "Those oysters were the most important evidence."

Oh, no! Noelle thought. Did that mean they could never solve the mystery?

Chapter Nine

"Why are those oysters so important?" Amber Lee asked. "Don't we have enough evidence?"

"We have some sand from Mr. Williams's oyster farm," Noelle said. "That's what Todd and I got."

"And we have an oyster from Mr. Spencer's oyster farm," Amber Lee said. "It's one that my mother bought."

"You're right," Dr. Smiley said. "But the oysters from Mr. Roper's grocery store are the 'disputed' oysters."

"What does 'disputed' mean?" Leon asked.

"It means that two different people claim the oysters came from them," Dr. Smiley said.

"Mr. Roper said he bought them from Mr. Spencer.

"Mr. Williams said Mr. Roper stole them from his oyster farm.

"If we don't have those oysters, we'll never be able to find out who's telling the truth."

Noelle knew that Dr. Smiley was right.

In fact, Dr. Smiley was always right.

That's why Noelle wanted to be like Dr. Smiley when she grew up.

She liked always being right.

When Dr. Smiley went back downstairs to her laboratory, Noelle said, "I have a plan!

"It'll mean we'll all get dirty, but that won't matter if we can keep Mr. Roper from going to jail."

Amber Lee looked suspicious. "What's your plan?"

"We'll surprise Dr. Smiley. We'll get the oysters back for her," Noelle said. "We'll dig them out of the garbage truck!"

"Yes!" Leon said. "I've always wanted to climb into the back of a garbage truck!"

"Oh, yuck!" Amber Lee said.

Noelle looked at her. "Police scientists have to get dirty sometimes, Amber Lee," she said.

48

"I think I'll stay here and answer the telephone," Amber Lee said.

"Why?" Todd asked.

"Todd!" Amber Lee said. "Police departments always have people who answer the telephone!"

"Amber Lee's right. We don't all need to go," Noelle said. "Leon, Todd, and I can do it."

"I put the oysters in a Smith's Department Store bag. It's bright yellow," Amber Lee said. "They're probably still inside it."

Noelle, Todd, and Leon raced out of Dr. Smiley's house and jumped on their bicycles.

"The garbage truck that picks up the garbage at Amber Lee's house also picks up the garbage at our house," Leon said. "I know which direction it goes!"

"How do you know that?" Noelle said.

"I've followed it before on my bicycle," Leon said.

They rode for several blocks.

They cut across lawns.

They raced down alleys.

Finally, they found the garbage truck.

It was parked in front of a small café.

49

"The garbage men know me," Leon said. "Come on. Let's go tell them what we need."

The garbage men were just coming out of the café.

"Hey, Leon!" they shouted to him. "What are you doing over here?"

Leon told them about the oysters.

"Well, we're not supposed to let people climb around in the back of the garbage truck," the driver said. He thought for a couple of minutes. "I know. We're on the way to the landfill now. Follow us. You can go through the garbage after we dump it out."

Noelle thought this was sounding worse and worse.

The smell that was coming from the back of the truck was beginning to make her sick.

Still, she'd never admit it. If Dr. Smiley could do it, she could do it.

Noelle, Todd, and Leon followed a safe distance behind the garbage truck as it drove the two miles to the landfill.

When they reached it, the garbage truck went through the gate to the side of a big hole and dumped the garbage.

"It's all yours," the driver said. He gave each of them a pair of old gloves. "Good luck."

Noelle, Todd, and Leon put on the gloves and started digging through the garbage.

"I really do feel like a police scientist," Noelle said. "I've seen them do this on television."

"This stuff stinks," Todd said. "I think I'm going to be sick."

"I don't smell anything bad," Leon said.

Noelle looked at Todd and rolled her eyes. Leon really seemed to be enjoying himself.

Ten minutes later, Todd shouted, "I see it!"

A yellow bag was stuck between two larger black garbage bags.

"I hope the oyster shells weren't smashed too much by the compacter," Noelle said.

Leon pulled out the yellow Smith's Department Store bag and opened it.

"Yeah! This is them," he said. "They look like they're in pretty good shape to me. I don't think the shells are broken."

"Good!" Noelle said. "Let's take them back to Dr. Smiley's laboratory!"

Chapter Ten

Noelle, Todd, and Leon raced back to Dr. Smiley's house.

Leon had agreed to hold the yellow bag of oysters.

Noelle was glad. She couldn't believe how awful it smelled.

She wondered if Dr. Smiley would even let them bring it inside.

She knew her mother would never let her do that.

When they reached Dr. Smiley's house, Amber Lee was waiting for them at the door.

"I'm glad I stayed here," Amber Lee said. "I answered the telephone once."

"We had to dig in a huge pile of garbage," Leon announced. "It was great."

"Ugh! I think I'm going to be sick," Amber Lee said. "You smell almost as bad as the oysters."

"Police scientists don't get sick, Amber Lee," Noelle said.

"Well, they try not to," Dr. Smiley said. She had come upstairs with Mr. Merlin.

Dr. Smiley looked at the yellow bag that Leon was holding. "What in the world is that?" she asked.

Noelle explained how they had recovered the oysters.

"I'm impressed. I was just about to call one of my assistants to do the same thing," Dr. Smiley said. She grinned. "I'm glad you didn't tell me where you were going, though. I would probably have said no."

"You three need to wash your hands, and then we all need to put on gloves and masks before we look at the evidence," Mr. Merlin said. "They'll protect us from germs."

When Noelle, Todd, and Leon finished cleaning up, they put on their gloves and masks and joined everyone else downstairs in Dr. Smiley's lab.

"We now have all of the evidence to solve this mystery," Mr. Merlin said.

"Everyone needs to stand at a microscope," Dr. Smiley said. "I'm going to make slides for you to look at."

Noelle and Todd went to the microscope they always used.

"Noelle and Todd got some sand from the beach in front of Mr. Williams's oyster farm," Mr. Merlin said. He helped Dr. Smiley hand everyone slides of the sand.

Noelle and Todd looked at theirs.

"What do you see?" Dr. Smiley asked.

"The grains of sand look like tiny planets," Noelle said.

"They have mountains and craters and everything," Todd added. "It's neat."

Everyone agreed.

"Study the sand carefully," Mr. Merlin said. "It's important that you remember what you're seeing."

Noelle and Todd took another look at the sand.

Noelle was sure that she'd recognize it if she saw it again.

Dr. Smiley held up a clear plastic bag. "This

is one of the oysters that Amber Lee's mother bought from Mr. Spencer's oyster farm.

"Now, who can tell me why this is important evidence?"

Noelle raised her hand. "There's sand inside the oyster shell!" she said. "So we need to look at it under the microscope."

"Right," Dr. Smiley said.

"I thought if a grain of sand got inside an oyster, it turned into a pearl," Amber Lee said.

"Good observation," Mr. Merlin said. "The sand Dr. Smiley found was just *inside* the shell.

"It hadn't got past what's called the *mantle*.

"The mantle is a membrane between the body and the shell.

"Sometimes a grain of sand can get through it.

"If it does, then it irritates the oyster.

"That's when the oyster turns it into a pearl."

Dr. Smiley handed everyone a slide.

Noelle and Todd looked at it.

That's strange, Noelle thought.

The grains of sand still had tiny mountains and craters, just like the sand from Mr. Williams's oysters.

But these grains of sand looked . . . *different.*

"Okay, Third-Grade Detectives," Mr. Merlin said. "What can you tell me?"

For a minute, nobody said anything.

Finally, Noelle raised her hand.

"Yes, Noelle?" Dr. Smiley said.

"They don't look like the other grains of sand," she said. "Why not?"

"Grains of sand from two different areas will be different," Dr. Smiley said. "When you compare them under a microscope, you can see that they don't look alike."

"They have different shapes," Todd added.

"Great work," Mr. Merlin said.

Noelle was really surprised.

When you were walking in sand, it all looked the same.

But if you looked at it under a microscope, it wasn't the same at all.

Suddenly, Noelle knew why the oysters from Mr. Roper's grocery store were so important.

"Let's look at the sand in the 'disputed' oysters!" she said.

"Yes!" the rest of the Third-Grade Detectives agreed.

Dr. Smiley handed the Third-Grade Detectives a slide.

"Look at it carefully," Mr. Merlin said. "Mr. Roper's future depends on what you find."

Noelle held her breath.

She looked into her microscope.

"Yes!" she cried.

The sand she was looking at now looked just like the sand from Mr. Spencer's oysters!

Mr. Roper hadn't stolen the oysters from Mr. Williams.

Mr. Roper had bought his oysters from Mr. Spencer.

The sand proved it!

The next day in class, the Third-Grade Detectives were happy.

When the sheriff told Mr. Williams about the sand, he was shocked.

Someone had been stealing oysters from him.

He set up a secret camera to take a picture of whoever it was.

It had worked!

He got a picture of the thief!

To Mr. Williams, the man in the picture really did look like Mr. Roper.

And the judge had agreed with him.

But they were wrong!

It was one of Mr. Williams's former employees.

The man had purposely dressed up to look like Mr. Roper.

"You've made Mr. Roper a very happy man," Mr. Merlin told everyone. "He's already back in his store, and he wants all the Third-Grade Detectives to come there after school today."

Everyone looked at each other.

"Why?" Noelle asked.

"He's going to give each of you a special treat for helping him," Mr. Merlin said. "And he's going to let you pick it out yourselves."

The class cheered.

Noelle knew that the Third-Grade Detectives would have helped Mr. Roper anyway. He was a very nice man, and he was their friend.

But if Mr. Roper thought he should give them all a treat, she wasn't going to say no!

Whose Lips Are Those?

One of the first things that the police look for at a crime scene is *prints*. Most people think they only look for *finger*prints, but they also look for *lip* prints. You may have seen lip prints on drinking glasses in your home.

Just like fingerprints, lip prints have special features that belong only to the person making the print. There are five common patterns of lip prints:

1. branching lines like those in the root of a plant
2. lines that form diamond shapes
3. rectangular lines that may crisscross
4. long vertical lines
5. short vertical lines

See if the detectives in your class can recognize somebody's lips! You'll need two days to solve this crime.

On the first day, choose six girls to make lip prints on a piece of paper. All six girls must wear lipstick of the same color. You can use one tube of lipstick and let the girls apply it with cotton swabs.

When the six girls have made their lip prints, the teacher will choose one of the lip prints to represent the one found at the scene of a crime.

On the second day, the same six girls will make one more print each and put their names on the prints. These will be left on a table at the front of the room. The detectives in the class will have to match the "suspect" lip print from the first day with the six lip prints from the second day.